JE
DRAGON
ALLIGATOR ARRIVED WITH
APPLES

FRIENDS
OF ACPL

P9-DZA-289

DO NOT REMOVE
CARDS FROM POCKET

ALLEN COUNTY PUBLIC LIBRARY

FORT WAYNE, INDIANA 46802

You may return this book to any agency, branch,
or bookmobile of the Allen County Public Library.

Alligator Arrived with Apples

A Potluck Alphabet Feast

by **Crescent Dragonwagon**

pictures by **Jose Aruego** & **Ariane Dewey**

Macmillan Publishing Company · New York

Allen County Public Library
Ft. Wayne, Indiana

Text copyright © 1987 by Crescent Dragonwagon • *Illustrations copyright © 1987 by Jose Aruego and Ariane Dewey* • *All rights reserved. No part of this book may be reproduced or transmitted in any form or by any means, electronic or mechanical, including photocopying, recording or by any information storage and retrieval system, without permission in writing from the Publisher.*
Macmillan Publishing Company, 866 Third Avenue, New York, N.Y. 10022 • *Collier Macmillan Canada, Inc.*
Printed and bound in Japan. First American Edition   10 9 8 7 6 5 4 3 2 1
The text of this book is set in 18 pt. ITC Zapf International italic. The illustrations are rendered in pen-and-ink and gouache.
Library of Congress Cataloging-in-Publication Data • *Dragonwagon, Crescent. Alligator arrived with apples. Summary: From Alligator's apples to Zebra's zucchini, a multitude of alphabetical animals and foods celebrate Thanksgiving with a grand feast. [1. Alphabet.   2. Animals – Fiction. 3. Thanksgiving – Fiction]   I. Aruego, Jose, ill. II. Dewey, Ariane, ill. III. Title.   PZ7.D7824Ak   1987   [E]   86-37   ISBN 0-02-733090-7*

Amanda C,
the very least
an aunt can do
is have a feast

With cakes and pies
in gooey pieces
and relatives,
especially nieces!

We'll have the family
A to Z
but first of all,
Amanda C!
                    —C.D.

To Juan
          —J.A. and A.D.

A feast for you
A feast for me
A feast that goes from A to Z!

A feast for us
and several guests
A feasting full Thanksgiving fest!

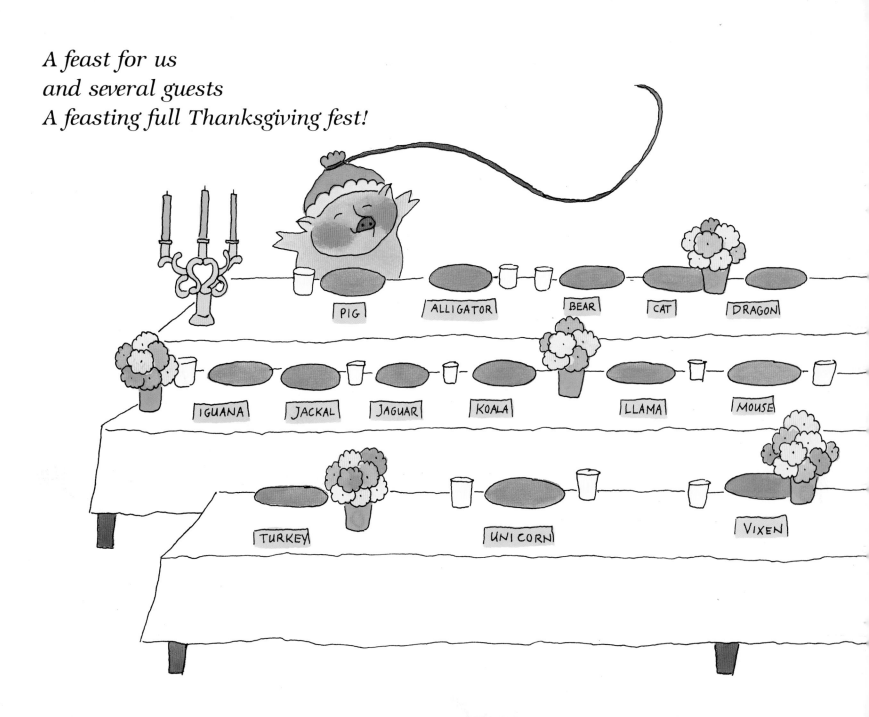

The table's full
Our friends are here
We'll eat from now until next year!

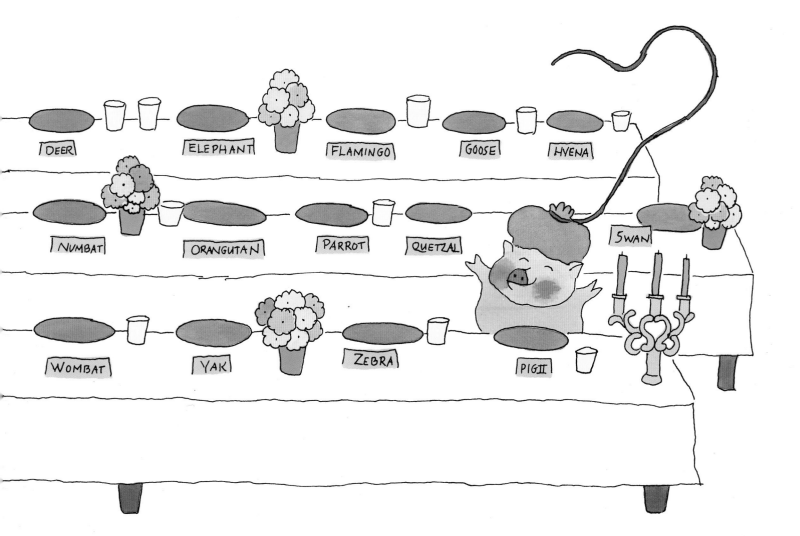

Alligator Arrived with
Apples And Allspice.

*B*Bear Brought Banana Bread, Biscuits, and Butter.

*C*Cat Came with Cranberry Compote and Cherry Cobbler.

D Dragon and Deer Diced Dates
and Delivered them to the Door.

E Elephant Eclipsed Everyone
with his Elderberry Elixir.

F Flamingo Found Fabulously Flavored
Fresh Figs and Fixed them Flambé.

G Goose Gave Gravy, Grapes, and Gingerbread.

H Hyena Had the Hiccups, but He Hailed us with Honey and Hazelnuts.

Hic!

Hic!

Hic!

Hic!

Hic!

I Indira of India Imparted Ice cream.

J Joe from Jerusalem Juggled Juices, Jams, and Jellies with Jaguar.

K Koala Kicked in Kale, Kohlrabi, and Kasha.

L Llama Lugged Lemons, Limes, and Lingonberries.

M There was Mocha Mousse
Made by Mouse,

N Noodles from Nick of Naples,

O and Onions and Olives Offered by Orangutan.

P Pumpkin Pie and Pickled Peaches were Provided by Parrot,

Q and there were Quinces from the Queen, **R** as well as the Royal Red Relish.

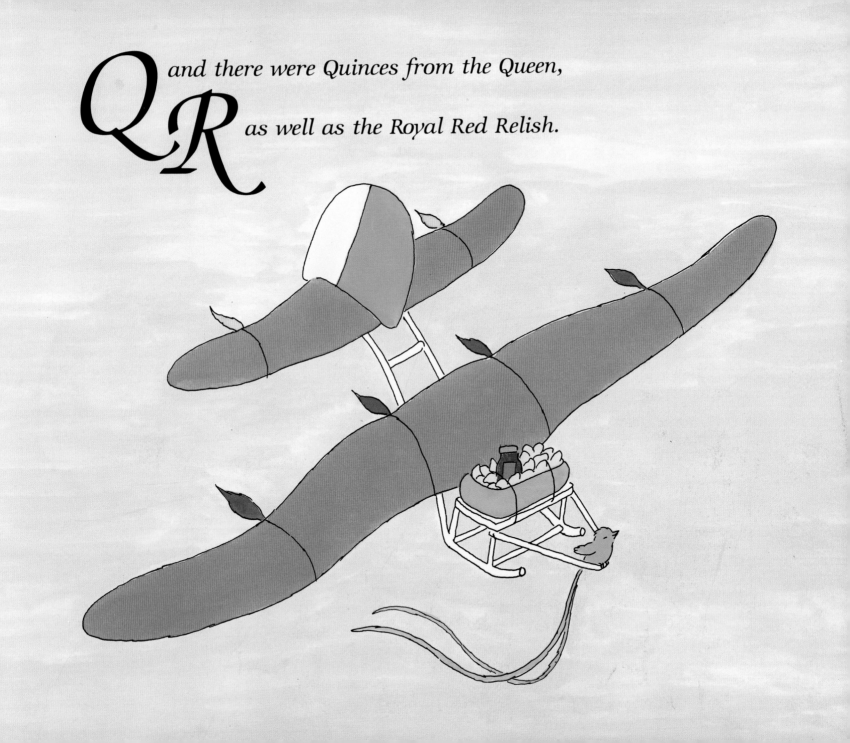

S *Swan Served Sage Stuffing and Squash Soufflé.*

T *Turkey Turned up with Tomatoes, Trifle, and Turnips.*

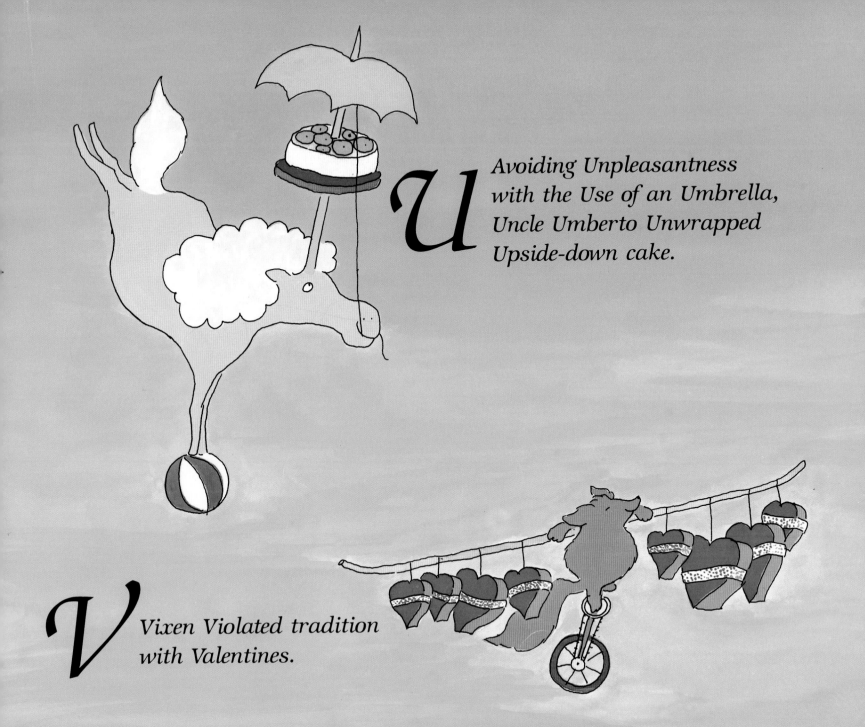

*Avoiding Unpleasantness
with the Use of an Umbrella,
Uncle Umberto Unwrapped
Upside-down cake.*

*Vixen Violated tradition
with Valentines.*

W Wombat Whipped up
Wild rice and Walnuts With Wine,

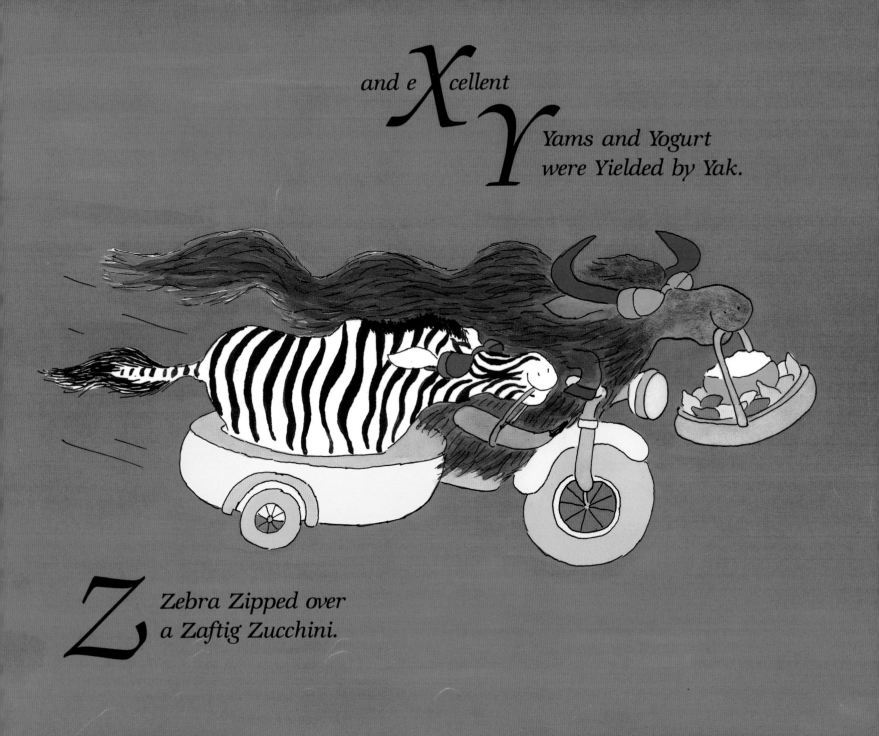

and e**X**cellent

Y Yams and Yogurt were Yielded by Yak.

Z Zebra Zipped over a Zaftig Zucchini.

We ate our way
from A to Z
Enough for you? Too much for me!

We ate so much
There are no scraps
It's time for our Thanksgiving naps!

Our sleep is deep
And many snore
When we wake up
we'll eat some more!

O thanks for friends
For food, for cheer
I'm glad Thanksgiving's once a year!

O thanks for friends
For food, for cheer
I'm glad Thanksgiving's once a year!

O thanks for friends
For food, for cheer
I'm glad Thanksgiving's once a year!

T3988